The Tempting Voice
A Mesmerizing Tale

by

Shivangi Sharma

Double 9 BOOKS

The Tempting Voice
A Mesmerizing Tale
by Shivangi Sharma

ISBN: 978-93-62202-42-0

Published by

DOUBLE 9 BOOKS
2/13-B, Ansari Road
Daryaganj, New Delhi – 110002
info@double9books.com
www.double9books.com
Tel. 011-40042856

ABOUT THE AUTHOR

Shivangi Sharma, a 28-year-old lawyer turned novelist, epitomizes the fusion of legal acumen and literary flair. With a fervent passion for writing, she has authored three books, showcasing her burgeoning talent and creativity. Armed with a postgraduate degree in Law, Shivangi is a natural writer, author, and poet by inclination. Her writing is imbued with a positivity and realism that resonates with readers, portraying her as a keen observer and compassionate storyteller. Through her work, she adeptly explores themes related to women's rights, politics, and humanity, with a focus on touching the soft and humane feelings of her creations. Shivangi strength lies in her honesty and integrity, evident in her fearless expression of opinions on issues concerning women and broader societal issues. She is unwavering in her advocacy for women's rights and self-respect, embodying a spirit of resilience and determination. As she continues to carve her path as a writer, Shivangi Sharma stands as a beacon of inspiration for aspiring writers and advocates alike, using her voice to effect positive change in society.

CONTENTS

Acknowledgements

- I would love to thank my parents and my grandmother for the impeccable support and unconditional love they showered on throughout my Journey.
- My special love to Megha, Shreya, Naman.
- I am extremely thankful to Rajat Gupta, my best friend, who gave me his immense support.
- Special thanks to my editor Mrs. Nupur Dhingra.

Prologue

In India, abiding by the rules of the society and impressing them is said to be the biggest task, but there is something tougher, being brought up as a girl child is the most difficult task of the society, Shanaya was one among them, being brought up in a conservative family prevented her from having much fun during her school days. A positive point to her life was the fact that she was the girl with dreams. She prepared for her examinations, worked hard to get admission to her favourite college to pursue her law in which she eventually succeeded. Little did she know that her life was only about to begin. She had a dream inside her head and realized that her dreams Flourished. She did not realize that another dream was getting planted inside her heart when she heard that mysterious voice that would change her life forever. She is going to live her destiny in a roller-coaster college days.

Love remains a desire when it cannot be fulfilled ever. This Novella is inspired by a True Life Story. It's a story of Shanaya and her journey in law college where she meets a guy named Aarav.

Chapter 1
The battle begins

Shanaya was sitting in her chamber and going through a case file. A sudden knock on the door diverted her attention. "Come in please," She responded and saw her junior approaching her table with a slip in her hand. She kept that in front of her.

" Ask the person to wait," She told her junior.

After a while, Shanaya removed her specs and kept them aside, took a deep breath. She stretched her neck and her eyes gazed at the hands of the clock which were reflecting 10:30 pm. *"Oh my Lord! I am late again."* She murmured and left her office hastily. She asked her assistant to switch off the light and lock the chamber while keeping a few files in her bag. "Ma'am, someone is waiting for you outside at the reception, I think you forgot that you have asked me to convey your message."

"Oh! No. This case made me forget everything. Send him inside, wait! Let me go out and apologize to him." She went out and a man was sitting in formal attire with a file in his hands and he was continuously looking at his Titan wrist watch tied on his left hand. She asked him with a quizzical reaction on her face, "excuse me?" The man replied, "Good Evening Ma'am, I am waiting for you since evening, a lady at the reception asked me to wait."

"I would like to beg your pardon here, I got indulged in studying a case and forgot that you are waiting here. I am so sorry, please come into my chamber and let me know how can I be of some help?"

"Ma'am I have come to you with sheer hope. It is a question of someone's life and death. I know it is too late but I beg you to please listen to me now. I will tell you everything in brief. But, please don't say no to me."

Shanaya could perceive his situation and asked him to explain the scenario.

"Ma'am, I am Prateek and I came to ask you to help and save my boss who is in trouble. None of the lawyers in this city is ready to take up his case, despite him being honest and genuine. When we were looking for a lawyer, someone suggested your

name to us and told us that you are a very promising and honest lawyer in this city.

"Can you please tell me the details of the case and why nobody is eager to take up this case?" Shanaya asked.

Ma'am, my boss is having a business of medicines and he marks his presence in the entire pharmaceutical sector. A few days back, we have placed an order for the material and a truck loaded the required material and headed to our storehouse. Meanwhile, on its way, it was stopped by the officials and got raided by them on the highway itself. According to them, they found some illegal drugs which are prohibited to sell in the market. When they asked for the license the driver could not produce the documents, because his job was just to transport the goods. The police have registered the case against my boss and arrested him overnight from his house. He showed all the papers to them but they were not convinced and the drugs which were being taken in custody by them did not belong to us." He took a pause and had a glass of water which was kept on the table."

He proceeded again, "Ma'am, Sir is innocent and he is unaware about that specific box which was lying there amongst the other packets. I am serving and working under him for the last seven years and he did not get involved in any such illegal activity. He is very clear and transparent. I have seen him working hard day and night and I am pretty sure that someone has laid a trap against him. Here are the papers." He showed her every minute detail regarding the case.

"Okay, Mr. Prateek, let me study this case file and shall discuss it with you tomorrow. We can fix up a meeting once I am done reading the file."

"Thanks, ma'am. I hope you will not disappoint me as everyone did. You are like a sparkling star of the darkest night. I will take your leave now." He left her office, and she left for her home.

After dinner, Shanaya went back to her room and laid down on her bed. She was so tired after the day and felt as if the slumber would take her in arms soon. On the contrary, she was unable to sleep that night. The scared and disappointed face of the client who came to her office that evening was flashing in front of her eyes. She felt a connection with that file which was handed over to her by Mr. Prateek.

She got up, and walked by the balcony, and sat on the revolving chair kept therein. The cool breeze was caressing her hair and the weather was a little cold. She brought the file given to her by that client and started studying that. The name of the owner choked her throat, left her eyes unblinking for a few seconds. The name of the owner who was behind the bars was, Aarav Malhotra. A name that was engraved in her heart, who gave her the memories for a lifetime. She got shocked, and hastily read all the information related to him. His address was showing the name of a beautiful city Dehradun, a place which was in her heart; which gave her wings to fly in this limitless sky. Her head got quizzed with so many questions but all of sudden, she releases the grip of the file and lost somewhere in memories of her college days.

Chapter 2
The voice

25th of July 2013

Nine framed certificates and a few medals were proudly flaunting on the wall along with the trophies exhibited on the brown wooden shelf, just behind the table of professor Gautami, revealing the eminence of the college in the field of education.

The affection of her, towards mother nature, could be perceived by the indoor plants which were kept near to the window at the left corner of that chamber.

Professor Gautami, a woman in her mid-forties, with black dyed hair, a blue neatly creased cotton saree with a monogrammed gilet, wearing silver-framed specs was sitting on the executive chair in her office.

Shanaya, a young, energetic, and bubbly girl was sitting in her office, discussing the necessary formalities like the College form, uniform, and so on, to get enrolled in the College.

"Ma'am, is it compulsory to wear the college uniform every day?" Shanaya asked.

"Yes Shanaya, what kind of questions is this?" Professor responded in amazement.

"I am so sorry Ma'am; I was just wondering that the uniforms were mandatory in schools only. By the way, I have filled up the form and attached all the documents like migration certificates, mark sheets, passport-sized pictures, and affidavits. Is there any document left that I need to attach herewith?" She asked.

"That's it, but I would suggest you, please go through the checklist once, before submitting your documents, apparently the signatures of your parents are left," Professor responded with a smile on her face.

"Sure Ma'am, I will get them signed today only and would comply with all the requirements mentioned in the checklist, and I would submit the form tomorrow positively, during the first half of the day." Shanaya reverted.

Take your time please, but make sure you submit them before the 30th of July,13."

Sure Ma'am, thank you so much."

Shanaya, a beautiful young girl, with a dusky tone and a lean frame but imbued with the innocence of a rosebud, having dreams and aspirations to become an eminent lawyer of the country, was filling the form to get enrolled in Dehradun National Law College in BA. LLB, which was situated on the outskirts of Dehradun, the capital of Uttarakhand. She was born and brought up in the pink city of India, Jaipur. Her family was shifted to Dehradun, as her father, who was providing his services to the income tax department, has got transferred that year to Dehradun. Becoming a renowned lawyer, after studying at a reputed college in the country was a dream since her childhood. She was from a conservative family, wherein girls were not allowed to study after attaining the age stipulated by Indian law to get married. But her dedication to studies, and becoming a professional forced her parents to allow her to continue further with her studies. But the way every new equipment comes along with an instruction manual to be followed, her permission to proceed with her studies popped in with the same instruction manual. "The friendship with the boys was strictly prohibited along with another condition of not bringing any of her friends to her place, unnecessarily."

All such things were going in her head, while she was putting the documents back in the folder. The thoughts running in her mind came to an end, on the spur of the moment when she heard a voice from her back.

"Ma'am, have you received the form along with the documents, that I have submitted to the peon to hand it over to you?"

"Yes! I have got them." Professor responded to that guy.

"Is there any kind of formalities left or should I leave?" He asked again.

"That's all for now, I have checked your documents, and you may leave now if we would require anything, we will ask you for the same," Professor told him.

"Ok, Ma'am. Thank you." He said with generosity.

That voice was silvery and was carrying sanguinity. She could feel so much positivity and cheerfulness in his voice. It was more like a melodious sound

coming from the flute of Krishna and she was engrossed like Radha. Shanaya was listening to their conversation as she was still sitting on the chair in front of her professor. Although she did not turn back to have a look at him; but she was desperate to see the person mastering that modulated voice. She could not hold herself more and turned to have a look at him but by then, he left the chamber. All she could see was a glimpse of his white formal shirt with grey dots on it. She closed her eyes in awe as if she had lost a trophy but there was something that belonged to her, went along with him. She felt like chasing him that moment only, but her etiquettes did not allow her to do the same due to the presence of Professor Gautami, and she glued herself on the chair.

After completing the formalities, she bade goodbye to the professor and left for her home which was merely 35 minutes from her college. She left for the home on her white-colored scooty.

While riding back home, she was smiling all the way. She could listen to that mesmerizing voice again and again. His words were roaming in her head like a beautiful melody and she was humming on its rhythm. She was incessantly thinking about him and was feeling a kind of attraction towards the voice.

Shanaya didn't know why she was feeling so delighted, but she was thrilled to share this gush of sentiments with her elder sister, Snigdha who was working in an IT firm in Mumbai. *Snigdha was also not an exception to that rule of TTBISP "Talking to boys is strictly prohibited".*

Shanaya decided to call her in the evening as her sister would be free to talk to her after office hours. As the clock struck 6, she dialed Snigdha's number and without asking about her well-being narrated the entire incident that happened to her in the morning.

"Di! Finally, I am going to *Dehradun National Law College and soon would become a law graduate from there. That day is not so far when you would have to make an appointment with my secretary to meet me. I am so happy!" Shanaya told her in excitement.*

"Really! That's great news... How about Mumma and Papa? How come they have agreed to continue with further studies?" Snigdha asked.

"Oh! Come on. Leave all that, I will tell you all this someday later. I need to share something else too."

"That I could sense, as you called at sharp 6'o clock, which happens only when you want to share something thrilling. Now blurt out fast," Snigdha said.

Shanaya stammered a little, "Today, mmm... actually, I was in the college today doing the formalities. Then...mmm, actually..."

"What happened to you? Now, you are getting onto my nerves. I can't wait anymore, please say." Snigdha asked.

She closed her eyes; kept her left hand's fingers crossed and said, "Today I met a guy. I mean, I heard somebody when I was sitting in the professor's office... I tried to look back but he was not there. I could only see his shirt." Shanaya said.

"Whom did you see? I mean could not see? And what's the big deal? Be clear." Snigdha asked her irritatingly.

"Di, I heard a voice that was so mesmerizing, and I am in love with that voice. I have never heard such a pleasant voice in my life ever before. I don't know whether he is a student or somebody's brother, I need to find him. I need to meet him once. Now I am desperately waiting for the 3rd of August to come so that I can see him, I mean hear him again. If he is the student, he would surely be there on the first day. I am keeping my fingers crossed. Only nine more days to go." Shanaya told her everything with delight.

"Are you mad or what? No need to get indulge in all this. Focus on your studies and fulfill your dream and don't forget the rule that we cannot break. Bye! I have some important work to do." And Snigdha disconnected the call.

Shanaya got disheartened after listening to her sister's reply as she was expecting her to listen to her with the same curiosity as she was having before sharing it with her. She went to her room and later had dinner as her mother had prepared her favorite noodles that day. She completed her dinner and went back to her room. She couldn't sleep properly that night, it was a long night. And, somehow passed nine days to wait for the College to open as it was her only hope to find that guy.

Chapter 3
The search begins

3rd of August

Finally, that most awaited morning has broken. The birds were chirping the beautiful melody. The gleam of the Sun was pouring the positivity and embarked the optimism of beholding the face that was behind that voice.

Shanaya woke up early than her parents that day. Although she was not an early riser, it was a day when her dreams were beginning to blossom. This could be one of the most amusing days of her life. She was still lying on her bed wearing a pleasant smile and was lost in her whimsical world, envisioning the looks of that guy whom she heard on the day of admission. She was wandering in the world of imagination, repeating those words told by him to the professor when her mother came to her room to make her awake for the day.

"Oh my God! You are awake, Shanaya! I need to check for the Sun's direction today." Her mother said with a sarcastic smile.

"Mumma, today is the first day of my college and I can not afford to get late, and I am a grown-up girl too." She responded with pride.

"I know this grown-up girl, from tomorrow I again need to make efforts to take you out of the bed. Now fold your linen, clean your bed, and get ready before you get late, as it is already 8 am." Her mother said and left the room.

Her eyes gazed at the clock that was mounted on the wall at her left and she ran towards her almirah to select the attire that she would be wearing that day. There was a dress code in the college but it was a perk for the first day, and students were allowed to wear casuals. She was a tomboy since her childhood and the makeup and flashy attires were not at all her cup of tea. But that was her first day in college, and she was a glooming bud who wanted to look her best amongst everyone.

She took out her favorite knee-length dress, but it was not ironed properly, then a white top with a baby pink skirt; but her watch was of rose gold color and it would look odd to carry it to her attire. Later a red top peeped out, and then a light grey formal shirt tried to make a place in her eyes, but nothing was working as she wanted to look splendid that day. All of her clothes came out of the almirah and were resting on the bed, expecting an opportunity to go out that day, but Shanaya was not able to pick one for her, and she closed her eyes cupping her face with both hands, "I don't have anything to wear."

All of sudden her mother came back with a black silky full sleeves shirt in her hands, "What have you done to your room Shanaya?"

"Mumma, I don't know what to wear for the first day, please help me."

"Snigdha called me in the morning, and asked me to gave this top to you, as she was aware that you won't be able to select one for you." Her mother handed her a black silk full sleeves shirt which was elegant and unique. Shanaya was fond of this black silky shirt but she never got a chance to wear this earlier.

"Aww, I love you my sister, mmuuhh..." And she hugged her mother.

"Now get ready fast and make sure you clean this mess before you leave the house." Her mother said and left the room.

Shanaya took the pile of all the clothes, lying on the bed and put them into her wardrobe, unfolded. She went to take the shower and came out in rush to get her hair done. She was not fond of makeup like other girls of her age, and the top and a pair of denim were her best buddies. Loose hair was something not her cup of tea and she used to tie them into a ponytail every time. She wore denim along with the black formal shirt; tied the laces of her black sneakers; stuffed her mouth with the breakfast and left her home in a rush.

While riding scooty to the college, she was wandering in her dreams of meeting that guy with silvery voice. Within no time she had reached the College.

The premises was full of colors, new faces, a few were chatting into groups and laughing out loud, while a few were glued to the notice board which was mounted on the wall in the corridor. Carrying a cute smile, Shanaya entered her classroom; that she had already seen on the day of admission.

A lean, dusky, and 5 feet 7 inches, jovial girl, was all set to step forth in the world of her dreams, to make new friends, to learn from everyone, to fill her life with a lot more achievements, and to make her father proud like ever. She glanced at every corner of her classroom which was jammed with the gossips, every seat that was occupied with the duffle bags; most of them were sitting on the desks; a few were flaunting their fashion sense while a set of girls were battling with fixing their hair and makeup too.

She entered the class and chose to sit on the second seat. Another girl was sitting quietly on the same desk. Shanaya, smiled looking at her and she responded with a beautiful smile. Her name was Mayera and she was a simple girl who was not interested in doing heavy makeup unlike other girls in the class. Later, she looked here and there but found herself amongst the strangers, all of them were present in the moment whereas, she was rambling in the thoughts of a guy behind that breathtaking voice. Although the values inculcated by her parents were there at the back of her mind, but she wanted to see that guy once.

All of sudden, silence prevailed in the classroom with the arrival of their professor. The class began with the introduction and ended on the same due to the higher strength of the students. Later on, three more professors came and began the session with the introduction only. It was getting very jaded and monotonous, giving an introduction again, and again. Moreover, getting relocated to that place was a reason that Shanaya had to answer a few more questions.

While in the series of forewords, she noticed a boy who was least interested in sharing anything about him. Every time he told his name only, and remain quiet despite asking a couple of times about him.

His name was Aarav and Shanaya felt as if he could be the one, she was looking for? Amongst the sixty students, her eyes stuck on him. Regrettably, she had no idea about his looks but she was hoping to find him someday. After the third session, she felt a bit thirsty and went to quench her thirst. The humid atmosphere was adding the spices of sweat along. She went out towards the water cooler which was kept around one fifty meters away from her classroom. She gulped it, and the moment she spun herself from there, a guy hoarded him back from the collision. She was naively staring at him with a smile on her face and he moved towards the water cooler. She said to herself in mind *"Thank god we didn't collide otherwise it would have become so embarrassing that too on the first day of college."* She came back to her seat and was thinking about Aarav, the guy who was making faces while giving his introduction and who was about to collide with her near to the water cooler.

After attending two more sessions, Shanaya left happily for her house after her first day in College. On her way back home, she was discerning about her first day. Everything that she liked or disliked, the students, the professors, a girl with whom she could share a smile, Mayera, but she was consoling herself to find that guy with silvery voice someday. She found

Aarav a little weird due to his behavior. He was cracking jokes; talking a lot with other students, but when it came to introducing himself, he remained quiet and was making faces that too in front of the Professor. And soon, she reached home and narrated the day to her mother.

She continued with her college for the next few days but was unable to make any friends, other than Mayera. The lectures have begun, and she had got occupied with her studies.

She always noticed Aarav used to remain in a group of four boys, and she was amazed by the soft skills that he became a center of attraction for everyone. It had been ten days since the college started, and she was comfortable with Mayera only. They both used to roam in the college together, chit-chatting during their break; sitting in the canteen, looking at the various groups which were forming in their class. She was comfortable with Mayera, rather than having numerous friends on her list, as she believed in the values and behavior of a person.

The College premises was massive having two canteens; one for the students and another one was for the Professors, specifically, a big basketball ground, football ground, badminton court, table tennis court were there as compared to the other colleges of Dehradun. It was located on the outskirts of Dehradun near jail road where the beauty of the hills was visible from the college's ground.

Dehradun was situated in a valley, surrounded by beautiful hills. Tea and maggie of 'Top View' restaurant of Dehradun-Mussorie road were very popular amongst the college students.

Shanaya was happy as she was cat-walking on her dream of becoming a lawyer. Her first semester studies were going well. She had five subjects in her first semester, and five professors to teach those subjects. Time was flying like that butterfly which was strenuous to chase. She was doing superb in her studies, but there was a distraction too. And it was not the voice that was magnetizing her since the beginning rather he was Aarav, who was entirely dissimilar to her. He was in love with breaking the rules, never came in uniform, moreover, was always laughing at something during the lectures.

Whenever Professors asked him to wear the uniform he politely used to say, "Yes Ma'am, sure thing from tomorrow."

He was an irregular student but was liked by everyone in the college, be it students or the Professor. His way of doing things was, as like as chalk and cheese, his language was not in his control, he never thought before speaking, with whom he was speaking, altogether he was blunt but somehow interesting.

He was a magician who could make smile anybody at any time. He had a charm in his eyes and voice. Aarav belonged to a Punjabi family he was quite straightforward, naughty, and a happy soul just contrasting from Shanaya. His dad was having a business Pharmacy for the last 5 years in the middle of Dehradun city. She over-heard all about him while he was narrating his family's background to one of his friends.

Shanaya was a sober girl, and politeness was in her blood, she was sophisticated and gracious. She was so particular about her words while Aarav could not survive without using foul language. Each line that came out of his mouth began with abusive words.

Days were passing by, she kept herself occupied with her studies and other activities in the college. Whenever her eye spotted a guy, her heart pondered a few thoughts and she started comparing his voice with that guy in her mind. She did not have a clasp on her heart and finally decided to find him anyhow. By the passage of time, the charm of the voice was intact, but the glimpses were fading away. She was not sure, whether she could recognize him by only listening to him. She was unable to find that guy by the end of the first semester.

From September 20th their mid-terms have commenced. She had got good marks in the internals. Everyone started preparing for the end semester that was about to begin in November itself.

Things were going well be it studies, projects, assignments but Shanaya always remained curious while looking at every other guy. But simultaneously she left the hope of finding him someday as he was nowhere. She could hardly recognize the boy and his *voice* even if he had come to the fore after so long.

Chapter 4
The observation mode: on

Shanaya took admission in August, and October was going on. She couldn't find a face behind that voice but couldn't forget him too. One fine day, she tried to speak to her Psychology professor, Gautami ma'am, indirectly about that guy.

"Good afternoon Ma'am," She stopped her from behind.

"If you don't mind, I wanted to ask you something." She asked sheepishly.

"Yes, Shanaya. How are your studies going on? I am sure you don't feel like a school-going girl now wearing this uniform! Okay, tell me what it is...I have to go somewhere so please be quick!"

"Ma'am, everything is going good and I am happy with the uniform too. The thing is, I am looking for a person in the college. Do you remember the day of counseling when I was filling my form sitting in your chamber, a boy entered the office to ask you something regarding his form? He mistakenly left his pen there and I am having it. So I was wondering to give it back to him, but I do not know his name. If you can help me a little?" She cooked a story out of curiosity.

"Mmm, no Shanaya, I am unable to recall any name as being a counselor almost every student approaches me for filling their forms and getting their queries resolved. So, I will beg your pardon here. And it is a small pen, you can keep it and give him back once you will find him. That's completely fine dear."

"I will take your leave now as I am getting late for my lecture, have a good day, and don't get panic about pitty things, you have a long way to go, focus on your studies!"

"Sure, Ma'am. Thank you for your time."

Shanaya was looking at her going, adjusting her folder and spectacles until she disappeared. A sense of secession was going through her nerves, and she felt like concentrating on her studies as accomplishing her dreams, was the only aim she came herein. She decided to forget that voice and moved on in her life. And after all, there was no benefit of hitting the bush.

She left for her class and tried to concentrate on the next lecture. While during the session, her eyes clogged on Aarav, who was busy doing something on his phone. A smile popped out on her face while the thoughts came out of her mind, "Don't know how he would be going to clear these semester exams."

During the last few months, Aarav made a place in everyone's heart. He had a sort of charm that nobody could ever avoid that guy of BA LLB class. Appearance-wise he was tall, handsome, smart, charming. The only thing Shanaya dislike about Aarav was his usage of foul language for no reason. He was a 6 feet tall guy, fair-complexioned with brown eyes.

She wanted to know more about Aarav, of which she could not understand the reason. But she started stalking him on Friends-book, and Vistagram, which were the most popular social platforms for youngsters. He was dragging Shanaya's attention since day one. He was that kind of a guy anyone could easily fall for. She was observing him since day one. His nature, behavior, dressing-sense, and everything else, but she never got a chance to talk to him. Her introvert and shy quirk along with the condition of her family were hindering her to become his friend, but she wanted to be his friend as to know more about him.

All of her Professors' considered Shanaya, a bright student, study was always been her passion. She always tried to be attentive during lectures but he was dragging her attention since day 1 of the college. She used to stare at him directly or indirectly. She knew that staring at someone was not her personality trait, but she was helpless. She often saw him in red-lined white socks and apprehended that, he was still a kid from inside and a smile appeared on her face whenever she had thought of him. Sneakers were his first preference and he kept on shaking his right foot during the boring lectures, he seemed to be a stubborn kid with a clean heart. He always used to sit on the middle row second bench whereas she liked to sit on the second last row third bench adjacent to his row.

Aarav was preferred by everyone, the way he dressed up and presented himself during the college demonstrations, and other events, his walking style, his confidence, and his charisma were stupendous. Soon he became famous in college. Everybody wanted to be his friend.

Soon, the Moot court Competition was announced in the college, which was going to be held on 10th November.

Chapter 5
The Intra Moot Court Competition

Shanaya was excited and thrilled to be a part of the upcoming Intra Moot court competition in the college. She was up with the articulation in her mind. Her enthusiasm was in full swing, she was geared up to win this competition as it was her forte. For the upcoming competition, she was reckoned to form a core team for the same.

She approached Mayera for the same with the anticipation of her being affirmative. But on the contrary, she refused to be a part of her core team as she was not comfortable with mooting, moreover, she wanted to focus on her studies only. Shanaya was a little gloomy that day and was unable to find someone else as Mayera was only her friend and the ray of hope. Further, she decided to take the advice from her professor Reema Ma'am. With the same intention, she headed towards her chamber and knocked on the door.

Reema ma'am was heading the co-curricular department of their college. She was graduated from one of the eminent colleges of Mumbai and was associated with this college for the past five years. This college has won so many awards and accolades under her supervision.

"May I come in, Maam?" Shanaya asked for her permission.

"Yes, please come in," Reema ma'am responded.

"Hello Shanaya, how are you doing? So good to see you here. I hope you are participating in the upcoming moot court competition." Reema ma'am, asked her cheerfully, adjusting her round spectacles.

"Yes Ma'am, even I am pretty excited and jubilated too. But I have come here for a little help from you."

"Yes, please tell me. How can I be of some help?" Ma'am reverted politely.

Reema ma'am was popular for her soft skills in college. Her aura was so positive and vibrant. She always used to carry a captivating smile on her face which was topped up by the dimple on her left cheek. Her love for silk sarees was perceptible from various colors of sarees that she never repeated.

"Ma'am, I am unable to fetch some students to form a team, could you please help me, by suggesting a few names to whom I can approach for the same?"

She kept her index finger on her forehead, thought for a while, and said, "You can ask with Abhikant and Aarav. They both are brilliant students with excellent records. I think, they would surely help you with this."

"Ma'am, are you sure about Aarav? I have never seen him serious with his studies and his attendance register speaks his tales of being lethargic."

"They both are having good communication skills, no doubt, Aarav would be requiring a lot of spoon-feeding. But he is exceptional when it comes to performance, just the spark is required." Ma'am told her enthusiastically.

"Okay Ma'am, I will speak to both of them and shall get back to you by tomorrow with the details of my core team for the competition.

Without wasting any time Shanaya first went to Abhikant.

Abhikant was a studious guy, who was encircled by books always. He was one such student who was always peeping onto the bookshelves of their college library. His bag was overloaded with books. His memory was too sharp, he was named Mr. Google in their college as he was super quick to all the queries, be it from the course books or any other book.

Abhikant was memorizing another book sitting on the first desk of their college library. She reached to him and whispered, "Hey, Abhikant, would you like to be a part of my core team for the Intra moot court competition? Reema ma'am has suggested your name to me for the same.

"I am extremely sorry Shanaya, I won't be able to take part in this upcoming competition. Although I want to, coming from a science background these new subjects like sociology and psychology are getting onto my nerves. I am facing trouble understanding them and need to take tutions after college hours. I hope you understand my situation." He responded making a puppy face.

"That's fine, no worries. The thing is I need two people to form a team for that, and Reema ma'am suggested your name. Don't worry, I will ask someone else." Shanaya told him hiding her frustration of not getting any affirmation till then.

Now it was Aarav's turn, and Shanaya was not sure whether he would agree or not, after all, he was a rockstar and they hardly spoke to each other. She headed towards the canteen where he could be hanging with his friends. It was already 4 pm and the college timings were over too, but she was determined to form a team before it is too late.

While crossing over the carpet of green grass that was laying in between, she found Aarav leaving for the day with his black and green coloured bag bumping up and down. He was delimited by three of our classmates and they were giggling over something.

"Hey, Aarav! Wait!" She wauled from his back, loud enough to stop him at once. *Her heart was beating fast while calling him from the back as this was going to be their first conversation ever. She was excited and nervous both at the same time.*

"There is something I want to talk about. I would be asking for a few minutes of your time and it is important for me." She asked for his permission.

"Yes Shanaya, how may I help you?

Shanaya replied "Reema ma'am has recommended your name to be in my team for the upcoming Moot court competition. Would you like to join me?"

"Amm..okay fine! But I would like you to add my friend Ryan to your team too as a Researches as he is excellent in his work and we don't do anything without each other, after all, we are good buddies."

"Alright, (without even thinking for a second) I don't mind Ryan joining in, as I need three to form a team of three members and no one has joined yet. Welcome to the team Aarav and please speak to Ryan once." She asked him as she wanted to get assured of all the members.

Ryan was a simple, sweet, sober guy with 5.6 feet height, who can be found in the library anytime. He was in the second year of the Bba LLB course. He was the topper of his class.

"Don't worry about him, he would not say no to me. You can count him in." Aarav told her with confidence.

After that Aarav left for the home. That was Shanaya's and Aarav's first conversation ever. Shanaya went back to her classroom, took her college bag, and left for home. She was too happy that day, maybe Aarav was the reason behind her happiness. She was flying without wings, swinging with the wind, warbling romantic songs, and was trying to whistle a little. Another reason for her exhilaration was the Moot court competition which was one of the fruitful events for her to showcase her talent in front of everyone. She wanted to win the trophy and blow the triumph of her success to the World, moreover, to her family who was conservative and wanted her to get settled in life. She was having that zeal streaming in her veins to prove herself to everyone who did not want her to continue with her studies further.

From the next morning, the preparation began and she thanked Reema Ma'am for her valuable suggestions. She was blossoming like a new bud on that day, the trio started working on it already. For Shanaya, it was not only a competition but a mark of success that she wanted to cross at any cost. And the cherry on the cake was the company of Aarav, whom she wanted to know since day one of her enrollment. He was having a magical charisma to attract people towards him. He was the favorite of everyone in the college, and due to her ordinary tomboyish looks, she never approached him to be her friend, but she wanted to. Behind the veil of this Moot court competition, she was getting a chance to know Aarav a little, what more she could have expected from her destiny. She was feeling a strong attraction with that guy from day one. Now she was accepting her feelings and was trying to be friends with him.

It was the morning of the 10th of October when she sent him the first text message on MYApp that, "Hi. Hope things are well at your end. We have to begin the preparations, so please be on time. And do ask Ryan too. It was a departmental library in the college premises where they have commenced the preparations for the competition. The preparations were going very well, Shanaya and Ryan were working hard on their memorials. Aarav was not that good in his studies neither he was focused on the competition. For the next few days they got busy preparing for the moot competition, Ryan and Shanaya did a lot of preparations for the same and their "Adda" was Library. Aarav used to bring Samosas sometimes and used to offer them to the Librarian also. They used to eat his favorite samosas together. Whenever Shanaya looked at him, she could fetch a strange silence hidden behind his words and smile, as if he was having a lot to share or maybe he was missing someone so badly. She could read in his eyes, but could not gather enough courage to ask him upfront. It could be his family issue or some kind of pressure to pursue the course he did not want to. There could be any reason behind his fake smile or maybe she was thinking too much about him.

Aarav never knew Shanaya's eyes were always on him, whether he was talking to somebody or doing anything, anywhere on the college premises. To notice him was the second favorite task of Shanaya during her college timings, and later on, stalking over his social profiles apart from studying.

20th October

It was a very special day for Shanaya. It was the day when her mother took her in her arms for the first time when she cried for the first time. Yes! It was her birthday. She was ecstatic to meet Aarav that day. She reached college before the time and wanted him to be the first one to wish her on her special day. Her eyes were stuck to the entrance of her classroom, everyone was coming one by one but her eyes were looking for him. She kept on waiting for him, keeping her fingers crossed. But at last her hopes got shattered when their Professor arrived and began with the lecture. Aarav didn't come that day. She gave a small party to everyone in the canteen, treating them with small patties and a coke, but she was missing Aarav that day.

The next day when he came, she was there at the library preparing for the competition. He went to her and asked for the party. She said, "I had given that yesterday, neither you came nor you wished me, so please forget the party."

"You don't know me yet Shanaya!" He said with attitude.

"Aha, do whatever you want to, I am not going to give you the treat today." She responded with buoyancy.

He bent forward, took her bag, and simply took 200 bucks out from the bag, and was about to go to Mac Donald's for buying the burgers and drinks for the party purpose. He was having his own Yamaha R-15 during the first year of college.

She was looking at him with question marks in her eyes and he asked her, *"Wanna come for a joyous ride?"*

But she denied and he went all alone to get the feast.

When he came back, his hands were stuffed with those brown envelopes which covered the burgers and fries, but she busts in laughter when he blinked his eyes as the coke was spilled all over his clothes and into the library too. She was laughing at him like insane. He was a Party Animal and cool dude in front of everyone, but she could observe an innocent child beneath a young clad! His weird things took her heart away, his smile was mesmerizing which made her blush always. She forgot the conditions on which her family gave her permission to study further. She began liking him a lot secretly.

It was the 9th of November when they were giving their practice a final shape, each of them was enthused with the winning spirit. Ryan was a quick learner while Shanaya had to work harder on Aarav. His silly talks, although she loved them, were the major hurdles on her way. She had to spoon-feed everything to him, that he was supposed to narrate. Their friendship was getting one notch up and each of them liked to be together. They bade goodbye on a happy note that evening.

It was around 9:00 pm when Shanaya had her dinner and was washing her hands when her cell phone buzzed. Her hands were wet, and before she could reach the plug point and detach that from the charging cable, her mother saw the screen.

"Aarav calling..."

"Shanaya, who is Aarav? And why is he calling at this time?" Her mother twisted her forehead lines, where numerous questions began appearing on the go.

Her father who was still sitting at the dining table gawked at her in amazement. They both were expecting her to retort, demanding an explanation.

"Mumma, he... he... is a classmate of mine," She spoke while stammering a little.

"But why is he calling you at this hour of the night? Shanaya. You know we don't like all this and we have already made it clear to you before getting enrolled in this college." Her father agitated on her adjusting his spectacles which were resting on his head.

"He is a classmate of mine, and we are a team representing our house in the Intra Moot court competition tomorrow. There is nothing like it as you are wondering. I am firm on my promises to you, believe me, I won't do any such thing which would break your trust." There was a confidence in her voice but a shiver in her body, as the back of her mind she started liking him.

She called him back as it got disconnected, due to the explanations demanded by her parents.

"Hi, Aarav! Is everything alright?" She asked him with a concerned tone.

"Hi, Shanaya! Yup, all well here. The thing is, I called you as Ryan was on-call with me, and wanted to talk to you too. He had to leave for his hometown due to some emergency with his family. His parents live in Rishikesh and he wanted to apologize to you for not being available tomorrow for the competition."

Her mind went blank for a while, she remained quiet as she was stunned to know that. She resumed herself and said, "I hope things would get fine with him soon." Her voice became dreary. "But, how would we manage without him? I wanted to give my best shot to this one. And, memorials are already sent to the head of the Moot court committee."

"Don't worry Shanaya, I am there with you," He said with ease and assurance.

The sheet of the gloom was disappeared from her thoughts when she found him by her side. She felt as if no one can stop her to blow the triumph tomorrow.

"Thank you Aarav, it means a lot to me. Listen, please come before time tomorrow, I will be waiting for you outside the college at 9'o clock."

The next morning, Shanaya went an hour before her usual time. She was glad to see Aarav, who was waiting for her to arrive.

"Hey, you came before me, great!" She said to him.

"I could sense some gloom encircling you last night. Hence, I am here to make you smile." He winked his right eye with a smile.

She smiled back at him and they tried to cover the part of Ryan and discussed the idea again to present it in such a way where they could fill the gaps.

At sharp 11'o clock, the competition began and they performed very well. But due to anxiety, nausea popped in and she was feeling like puking over the stage. Aarav could sense her worry and calmed her down a couple of times. Everyone could sense her situation sitting onto the Jury's desk or into the Moot Court, but they somehow managed to perform up to the mark without Ryan.

"I am scared of the results dude, I am pretty sure about our defeat today." She spoke in despair.

"Shanaya, we have given our best shot, despite the absence of Ryan left in between. The vital thing is, we have not left the path of courage and did whatever we could. So relax! Let us not think about it much. Have some water, it will make you feel better."

Shanaya was lost in her web of thoughts. She has never seen this amazing side of Aarav before. She was so happy that he was concerned for her. She had goosebumps. She was smiling for no reason, and all of sudden came back to her senses when she heard the name of the winning team.

The team that has bagged the first position is "SHAARAV". It was the name they had given to their team once Ryan left them in between. And she could not believe her ears. Yes! They won that competition and everyone was applauding them. The day ended with happiness on her face and pride in the eyes of Aarav too.

During the first year of college, Aarav used to be the popular face as he was good-looking too, who was the crush of many girls in the college. While Shanaya was a simple, sweet, boring, shy, and introvert, girl. Her skin tone was dull. Aarav always used to call her by the name 'Laughing Budhha'. Things were going well in the first year they even won an English Quiz together. Aarav became Shanaya's desire, an unavoidable desire.

Chapter 6
The College Event and Shanaya's dreams

February approached soon. It was known as the month of love as Valentine's day was in a row. Apart from that, the college fest was there in the same month which was perfect for everyone to enjoy, prepare for various activities, to showcase their talents apart from studies in cultural activities.

Students have started preparing for the college function, a few were bunking their classes in the name of preparing for the college day. And professors were also giving them that freedom to enjoy during the fest.

Results of the first semester were out and Shanaya became the topper of her class. Everyone was asking to throw a party as she stood first in the class. She was joyful as she could be able to perform up to the mark and expectations of her parents. She needed to score good marks to show her capabilities and determination to everyone. Now everyone knew her by name in the college, unlike earlier when nobody knew her.

She even threw a pizza party for her classmates including Sami, Mayera, Aarav, Mishthi, Ryan, etc. in the college with the help of Aarav after the lectures got over. She ordered the pizza from Aarav's favorite pizza outlet. Shanaya and her friends danced to the music for the next few minutes and then the party got over. This was the first time when Aarav saw Shanaya dancing like an angel. The day got over with big smiles on everybody's face, especially on Shanaya's face as Aarav contributed some money for the pizza party.

Shanaya was focusing on her studies and did not want to participate in the college event but her classmate Mishthi insisted on her. Mishthi was a good dancer, she used to give dance coaching to the kids who used to live nearby her house. Mishthi convinced her to perform along with her and finally, she had to say yes to her wishes. They both prepared a song named, "Mujhe to teri lat gayi" from the Bollywood movie Race.

On the day of the college event, Mishthi couldn't participate due to her father's bad health. She had to take him to the hospital and Shanaya had left with no other choice apart from performing alone. It was the 27th of February, a night before the event she couldn't sleep for the whole night as she was too excited to wear a saree for the first time in her life that too for a college function. Everyone was wearing sarees or suits on that event night. The next day she woke up early in the morning, got ready for college, and reached before time. She was very nervous that day as she had to look her best. Aarav would be seeing her in saree for the first time. Her mother, and Snigdha who came for a couple of days to Dehradun, helped her to wear a saree and look her best. She was more like a tomboy who kept a distance from all kinds of makeup products and looking like a girl was a tough task for her. She asked her father to drop her before leaving for the office. His father's office was 15kms away from their house. She was nervous on the way to college.

She stepped out of her father's car and waved him goodbye. She was moving slowly and steadily with grace towards the entrance, adjusting her open traces and the border of the saree, as she was anxious about her looks that day. All of sudden, a voice shrieked and all she could hear was, "*Shanaya achi lag rhe ho*!" By the time she turned back to see the face behind that voice, he disappeared. For a moment she felt as if it was the same voice she heard on the day of enrollment. Her heart skipped a beat. She had that urge to find him anyhow earlier, but she thought that he was not a part of that college and she almost forgot about him. Murmuring from herself, she was looking for Aarav everywhere in the college premises as she wanted him to see her once. After all, she put on makeup for the first time, her eyes were searching for him.

Her eyes could not spot him anywhere and she was standing near Mayera and were discussing the time taken to wear a saree for the first time. All of a sudden, Aarav joined them and started the conversation with Mayera. Shanaya was expecting a compliment from him that day and was looking at him once and then on her saree, further repeating this a couple of times, just if he could notice her in a saree. She tried to divert his attention towards her by adjusting her saree but he did not say anything and kept on talking with Mayera over something related to college activity to be happening soon.

Mayera noticed Shanaya's anticipations and she could not resist herself by saying, "Won't you compliment Shanaya on her attire today?"

Shanaya felt like slapping Mayera for that, but Aarav replied *'I have already complimented her when she was entering the campus.'*

Oh Gosh! She said to herself " *It was Aarav who told those words to me, and I was wondering about that guy of mesmerizing voice, why did not I recognize him?* while thinking this her face blushed and became red like a tomato.

Later on, she was biting her nails, and rubbing both hands together simultaneously as the stress was heading on her mind. That day she had to dance in front of the crowd, dancing was one of her hobbies since childhood. But she never felt such kind of edginess, before.

Soon her turn has come and she performed more than what she was expecting out of her. She performed well according to her seniors and friends, but one thing was bothering her whether he saw her dancing her or not. She even sang one of the old numbers as Mayera insisted on her. Mayera also got an opportunity to sing her favourite song in front of all her classmates for her crush.

The event went so well and ended with a delightful dance of students and professors. She couldn't find Aarav afterward, that day Aarav left early for the home. That day ended and Shanaya went back home, as one of her friends dropped her.

she could never ask him whether he listened to her singing or dancing that day. Aarav was having a part-time job too, and he remained busy sometimes with his job, his dad's pharmacy business, and the rest of the time with his friends. He was not a regular guy he used to come on alternate days in the college. He was a guy with a good IQ level, smartness, and intelligence. He possessed all the skills that can make him a good businessman someday. She always knew he would be on top of this world one day in the future. Her likings for Aarav was increasing day by day. That day Aarav was looking stunning in a black blazer, no one can ever beat him in looks. He was everybody's crush including her.

Chapter 7
Dreams and Aarav: A soul connection

Shanaya was doing great with her studies and became a known face in college. The students who used to bunk the college, came to her so that they could copy the notes from her work. She loved to help everyone, but her most favorite task was doing something for Aarav. He remained out of the class most of the days and took the help of Shanaya by copying her notes so that he could study at the last minute. Everything was normal with her to expect for the one. She used to dream about Aarav every time, every day. Sometimes Aarav was holding a rose in his hand to propose her in front of the whole college, sometimes to help her from the eve-teasers, a couple of times they were sharing the same drink with two straws, or she was sitting on his bike showing off with pride teasing the other girls in the college. She loved to imagine him every moment with her, in college or after that. Maybe these were her desires that wanted him every time to make it memorable and mesmerizing. She observed his style and everything about him since day one and tried to speak like him in front of a mirror, confirming no one was noticing her. Her fancies kept on hooking from the beginning and continued for so long. She felt their soul was connected somehow, she could feel that spark in his eyes. Whenever he looked at her, she used to blush and look downwards. Those days of practicing for the Intra Moot court competition were so alive in dreams. When their hands got touched, their eyes met, when he offered her to be her companion till the Mac Donald's for getting some feast, when he helped her win the competition despite Ryan left in between. She imagined her future with him too, the wedding rituals, the flashy attire, the bridal things were all her companions in her fictional world.

Maybe they were the soul mates made for each other. If Aarav was around her, she became speechless in front of him. She found herself blushing without any reason all the time. She often behaved so dumbly in front of him and he knew very well that she was smart enough to hide her emotions in her smile. She could feel some vibes from Aarav too, and she wished that he would surely understand her someday. They used to play badminton with each other for hours as it was their favorite game at that time. Shanaya always tried to steal her eyes from him so that he would not notice him while seeing him. She didn't know whether he noticed her or not she could never ask this thing from him. They used to play Ludo, Dramsharas, Current pass, Truth and dare, and many more indoor games like that during free lectures and recess. Shanaya never dared to say no for playing any of the games, in fact, it was Aarav who used to drag her in his group of friends. She had only two to three friends including Mayera, Sami, and Aarav during the first year of college. Aarav always wanted her to speak more and to play more with him maybe because of this she started getting wrong signals from him.

They never met on a date officially, to hang out together but they always conversed on calls, and messages, but only regarding work, studies, his friends, his job, etc. In the first year, he used to call her and narrate the tales of his love life and how crappy his girlfriends were. He told her everything about them and their behavior. And she was so fond of him that she listened to everything calmly despite having no interest in any of his talks about his chicks. She wanted to be with him and for the reason used to hear from him. They never spoke about their relation or friendship except on the 22nd of October, 2014.

Once they went to the National Law University Dehradun to participate in sports in the fest named "Aan Ban Shan" together. Shanaya was thrilled to be somewhere along with him outside the college too. She came to the college and followed him along with her senior Meera who was also participating in the fest. They both were on her scooty but did not know the way to the NLU. Aarav guided them about the way and they enjoyed their journey of around an hour together. When they have reached the University, she got to know one more secret about him that he was fond of chess too and he was participating in a chess competition in that fest. His keen interest in that game had generated the interest of Shanaya towards the same and she began learning chess at her home too, in fact, she asked her father to make her master that game with the thought of playing that game, sitting opposite to him someday. He had awesome chess skills. Her friend Meera was a national-level badminton player and she inspired Shanaya to participate in the competition.

The competition was about to begin. They were excited to play the game at one notch above the level. Aarav and Shanaya both greeted each other, said "*Best of Luck*", and went to different areas according to their respective games. The luck was not following them that day, as any of them could not win the game despite giving tough competition to their competitors. They both have lost at the game points and Shanaya considered it as one more similarity between them. The competition had ended in the evening after the valedictory ceremony. Shanaya was so happy spending a day out with her ideal partner, in the beautiful valleys of Dehradun. They all went back to their home as it was 6 in the evening. Shanaya dropped Meera at her home on her white-colored scooty and headed towards her house. She was thinking at the back of her mind, "The day was not good but it's a part of life, sometimes we win, we lose, it's not in our hands. Participation is important than winning.

Aarav was a gentleman he never did anything or said anything that is not appropriate for a girl though he had many Girlfriends in his past. He always used to keep a distance from the girls. He never liked to talk to the girls except for the group conversation. Shanaya wanted him to give her some extra time but could never ask for it. She wanted to spend time with him but he always used to keep running from her. After the college first year, Aarav made a few friends who were girls. One girl named Salvi was getting close to him as a friend. Salvi was a tall girl with good features, she belonged to the Bhimtal. Shanaya personally never liked their friendship as she knew the intention of that girl. Aarav and Salvi even went to hang out together but Shanaya was an introverted girl she always had a fear of spoiling her image as a good student in going out with him alone in the eyes of seniors and her professors, although she wanted to hang out with him. He even asked her twice in the first year to come on Dandiya nights and to watch a movie but she denied it as she knew this will invite rumors about her and him. And above all that her conservative family will not allow her to go and enjoy her life that too after 6 in the evening.

Chapter 8
"Good Friends Mode: On"

Shanaya was in love with college life. On one hand, she was walking on an aisle towards her dreams and on the other side, she was learning the meaning of life living with happiness with someone who was making her blush every day.

She was so happy and friendly with Aarav. They both used to laugh at silly things together, hanging around with each other in the college canteen, running behind each other to hit while teasing each other, winning various competitions while participating together. Everyone instigated assuming them as a couple though they were not. They became good friends those days. Shanaya was enjoying their friendship and she used to help him out with his studies, assignments, projects, presentations. In a law college, they both had a lot of burden of studies. Things were going on track even professors started talking about them, if these two were sitting together the full class used to stare at them by turning their necks all the time. They used to answer a lot during lectures together and argue without any reason.

She forgot about the "TTBISP" rule of her family. She wanted to know the reason behind that strictness in her family. No one amongst her friends in the college was having such restrictions on them. She felt a little bounded. The goodness of Aarav was provoking her to speak to her parents about their so-called rules. She wanted to break those barriers and fly in this limitless sky with her dreams and a partner who would always remain by her side. She never understood why her parents protected her from being with boys. She was very happy with the one she has chosen for her. Deep down somewhere she wanted to prove her parents wrong about their perception towards boys. But the bond she was sharing with Aarav could only be understood by her heart, she could never discuss her emotions with Snigdha too. She wanted to be assured about the feelings of Aarav towards her. And the same ways her life was going on…

Although Aarav was a cool guy he was behaving a bit caring for a couple of days, he was asking a few things about Shanaya from her friends. Most of the time she remained lost in her thoughts resulting in her being quiet sometimes. And for the same reason, Aarav kept on asking about her well-being, and the reason behind her such behavior. He was wondering that she was in a bad mood while she was lost somewhere in weaving her future with him. But in between all such things, she was jovial that he was concerned for her, and the change in her behavior made him think about her a little more.

Some of her friends including Mayera, Sami told her *"Maybe Aarav likes u too,"* and she should confess her emotions for him before it is too late. Sami was their other friend who took the admission a bit late in the college. She was a little dusky and was having a lower IQ level. Shanaya had shared her emotions for Aarav, with three of her friends; Mayera, Sami, and Riya. Riya became Shanaya's good friend in the second year itself. They all had discussed her sentiments the other day in college, for that they have skipped their lecture and sat together to make some plan to help their friend. According to them, they would convey Shanaya's emotion in such a way that it would reach Aarav without being confessed by Shanaya as she was a little shy and scared to share her heart with someone. Aarav was a smart guy so they all will be talking to him in her place. Shanaya got to agree to this stupid plan made by her friends and started waiting for the right day when her feelings will be told to Aarav through her friends. It was Mayera who used to tease Shanaya a lot whenever Aarav used to enter their classroom. It was her work to start singing the same song on repeat mode "tune mari entryan dil me baji ghantiyan". Shanaya used to start blush like hell.

A few days later, they were supposed to arrange a fresher's party for their juniors in the college. Aarav took the responsibility of managing the entire event. He was planning for the performances to be done, collecting the amount from the students, sending invites to them in a creative manner, and so on.

Aarav was not a guy who can trust anybody so easily. He even never liked to make friends instantly but due to his flexible nature, everybody in the class wanted to become his friend. As he wanted someone trustworthy for handling the cash received from the students for the party, he asked Shanaya if she could help him with managing the collections Having immense faith in his beloved friend. Shanaya took the responsibility on her shoulders with pride, due to the reason as Aarav bestowed the trust upon her. She collected the amount from all the students within a span of two days and Aarav got impressed by her skills. She handed over the amount to Aarav the next day as her Moot court competition was also approaching the coming month, and she had to practice for that too. She did not want to leave any loophole this time like that of the first time when she was herself a fresher. She hooked herself with practicing for her part in the Moot court competition and for the rest of the time, she kept focusing on her studies. She composed herself that ways where she could be able to prepare for her competition, fresher's evening and her studies too. Her level of enthusiasm was unbeatable and she managed everything calmly.

18 August 2014, the day had come for which they were excited and thrilled for a few days; which was Fresher's eve. Shanaya still remembers that she couldn't attend her own freshers in 2013 so she decided to look mindblowing this time. That day Shanaya decided to wear a WhiteGown. She wanted to surprise everyone in the college with her elegance. Her inclination towards Aarav was creating wonders and she became sophisticated towards her choice of attires. Her family could feel the changes in her but they remained quiet as they wanted her to blossom as she wished. She had got ready by leaving her hair open, wore very less makeup on her face. The silver-colored long white diamond earrings were going superb with her attire which she tried for the first time in her life bought for her by her mother. Her ponytail went away with the time and her loose traces were dancing on her shoulders, the sneakers were peeping from a corner but she wore heels that day. Lastly, she applied a perky pink lip gloss on her lips and was all set to rock the floor with her stunning looks. She was looking at herself in the mirror when her mother entered her room, *"Wow! You are looking splendid Shanaya."*

The Smile on her cheeks widened as she received her first compliment. "Thank you, Mumma."

She kept herself dressed simple with a touch of elegance, as she was a shadow of her mother only. She taught her that simplicity was best and when it was about applying makeup, she told her that, *'A girl's real beauty lies in her simplicity.'*

The moment she reached the college, all eyes were halting at her, everyone was looking and complimenting her that day as the tomboy was molding herself into a sophisticated version. She was so delightful after so many compliments that she received and was eagerly waiting for one such compliment from someone special who transformed her that way. When she entered the college campus and stepped in towards the party hall he was also coming from the other side. He left his mouth open with his big eyes. After, that she couldn't find him for the next one hour. Her eyes were looking for him everywhere but could not find him there on the premises. Later, she had reached backstage, where he was managing the show. He looked at her, "Hey! Shanaya, thank god you are here. Please, have a look and confirm whether everyone is ready to perform with their props or not?"

She was looking at him with a question mark on her forehead, she did not blink her eye in anticipation of missing any signal of praise. But when he opened his mouth, he said, *"What happened to you? Why are you looking at me like this? Come on, we are left with very little time."*

"No, nothing. Let me check everything." She said in a dull tone as she was expecting him to compliment her on her looks that day. She engaged herself in the work and left from there.

During the fresher's evening, the host of the party was Amit, and he was the one anchoring at the stage too. He mastered everything that evening from planning to executing the events. Aarav helped him in managing the show. His confidence was superb and the way he was handling everything was out of this world. One amongst other activities included a prize for the best-dressed girl. Amit announced her name while she was seated amongst the audience for winning the maximum votes for being dressed gracefully that evening. The prize was given at the stage by the Dean of their college, and Aarav was standing beside her while receiving that. She was so happy to bag a prize and once opened there was a cute sling bag therein.

Everyone applauded her sophisticated and graceful attire, but Aarav did not say any single word of appreciation.

The bashfulness of Shanaya was taking her back to confess her emotions to him, but his ignorance was bothering her too. She kept on dreaming about him all the time, but could not gather enough courage to accept her heartfelt sentiments. But the time was fleeing like a butterfly which was tedious to catch. She did not want to be only a friend of him, rather wanted to get a tag of something beyond that. She wanted to live with him in her dreamworld with love all around, his care and affection ceiling the sky, she wanted to spend some more time with him, and it would not be contrasting to say that she wanted to spend her life with him. Her feelings were growing every day, and she forgot about that voice too which was hypnotizing her during the first year. All she wanted was his company and affection. Hence, she decided to tell share her heart with Aarav by professing her emotions in front of him that evening.

She was looking for an opportunity to be with him for a while in person, away from the crowd, but was unable to fetch his time as he was preoccupied with his chores to be performed on time. But she believed that if she wanted to do something, she had to chase it till eternity. And she had got a chance once the party was over and she proposed to him, to dance with her. An offer he could not refuse, he said yes and they started dancing on the floor. Although the song was boring enough to perform on the beats. Shanaya was delighted to see him that close to her. While dancing, her gaze shifted on Mayera, who was looking at both of them sheepishly and teasing Shanaya by making faces and signs of love birds. Shanaya blushed after that and the moment her eyes met with Aarav, he left the floor in between as he was not comfortable with dancing with a girl for so long.

She tried to follow him but her gown stuck into her bellies and she had to stop to fix that problem. That day ended with a big smile on everybody's face. But Shanaya was lost in her world and was trying to spill the quantum of her emotions on him as she was not having enough space in her heart to bottle them in.

She took a deep sigh and followed him backstage with the confidence to pour out every hidden emotion out on him. She heard him talking to someone over the call and she held herself for a while to wait, till he finished his conversation. She was standing a bit far from him and was unable to hear the conversation. *Although her values did not allow her to stand a little closer and listen to the conversation but deep down somewhere, she was keen to see him free soon. The moment she put a step forward, she heard the name* "Kayra". She could not proceed further as Kayra was the girl who was in a long-distance relationship with him.

Her reticence overshadowed her again, and she refrained herself from proposing to him that evening. She dropped the idea of telling her feelings to Aarav and went back to her home after the function got over.

Later during the night when she was lying on the bed on her stomach, she thought, another day has gone without him, she was having an opportunity to express herself but could not do so." *That pain was unbearable for her. She wanted to confess her feelings but he was already committed. Yes, he was in a relationship with a girl for many years. She was in a dilemma about what to do next? She should tell her feelings to Aarav or not? What he will think about her? She already asked her friends not to share anything with Aarav as it will not look good and Aarav will judge her for this. In the end, she was questioning herself, "Has she done the right thing as she decided not to disclose her feelings to him.*

Chapter 9
Her Birthday

20th October 2014

It was another day for everyone but an imperative one for Shanaya. It was her birthday and she was at home till now. Apart from her birthday, there was a Moot court competition also. She was preparing for this competition for so long and was confident to win that too. But unfortunately, Varuna who was also participating along with her this year had refused to participate this year due to the sudden fixation of her sister's marriage and which would be happening in the next 10 days. She had canceled her plan to participate in moot court as it will take a lot of days. She was a girl who used to plan everything before executing and it was on her topmost priority list to participate in at least three Moot courts that year. Her day began with sad news and she decided to stay at home. Her parents went out of Dehradun for the day But she called Mayera and Riya to be at her place as she did not feel like staying alone with her thoughts and gloominess.

Therefore on the day of her birthday, Shanaya was upset and waiting for Mayera and Riya to come home so that they could talk at least. Shanaya was expecting the two of her friends at any moment when the doorbell rang, and she ran towards the door she was amused and stunned to see her friends there. Near to twenty of her classmates came to her place with the props, cake, gifts, balloons, and birthday caps too. A loud voice clinched her ears when saw them all together. They began to sing, "Happy Birth Day, Shanaya…"

Her eyes froze on Aarav, who was also a part of the surprise team and that was a pleasant surprise for her. It made her day so beautiful with something like a dream come true. She was dancing without music, her heart was pounding louder, she wanted to run towards him and hug him tighter. She was on cloud nine, could not believe her eyes for a moment. Her gloom disappeared in a bleak and she felt like, "life is beautiful with you by my side." Somehow she controlled her emotions and came back to normal.

She invited them all inside her house, and they all entered with smiles and happiness on their faces. They all were so happy and cheerful, like the kids who were excited to get the invite and were imagining the party, with cake and balloons.

"Happy Birthday Shanaya…Happy Birthday, dear.." Everybody started wishing her. Aarav also wished her. They had brought a cake, and gifts for her. Shanaya cut the cake and thereafter they all partied together, they sang songs, dance to the latest numbers, had snacks that they had brought along, and played a few games together to make her feel better. Shanaya's eyes were on Aarav only. She was observing him, and all of his activities, and funny gestures. She felt like a sense of belongingness to him. His presence in her house made her feel out of the world and she was humming on her own tunes. She noticed him puffing his mouth with the snacks, having a competition with his friends. His innocence made her fall for him once again. She observed every bit of him and thought of his innocence and a kid who was hidden beneath the tag of a cool dude. He pretended to be an insensitive guy every time. He did not care about his past girlfriends. He never spoke about them, but Shanaya could perceive the other guy who was hiding him under the cover of a rocking guy. She was enjoying every minute of her birthday being surrounded by Aarav.

After celebrating her birthday at her place and gifting her a marvelous surprise, they all went to Burger King which was 2km away from her house. They all were riding bikes and scooties were following the guys as if some rally was going on. They enjoyed every moment and departed for their homes from there only. The most exciting part of the day after Aarav was that, they all bunked the college that day, just to make her feel special on her birthday. The day ended with big smiles all around. Shanaya was too happy and excited as she got her first picture with Aarav on her birthday. This was also one of her bucket list's desires.

Shanaya always wanted to sit on his bike, It was the 19th of November when Aarav wanted some notes from Shanaya. She asked him to collect the notes from her from a nearby location as examinations were approaching. She handed him all the notes as required by him. He asked her to sit at the back on his bike and he wanted to gift her a ride as she helped him a lot at the last minute before the examination. She could not refuse that offer by him and sat on his bike for the first time. It was a wow feeling for her. She sat crossed legs and kept her right hand on his right shoulder. She felt like he was taking her to his world. The cool breeze was touching her hair, her ponytail was dancing in the air. She wanted it to be a never-ending ride. She always wanted to spend time, and roam around the world with him all alone. She wanted to explore the relationship, they were sharing. They had a weird relationship that was not expressable in words. He gave her all the signals but never confessed his emotions for her, being a shy girl could not propose to him for the relationship.

The next day when Shanaya reached college, her friends started to tease her as, "Shanaya when would you be confessing your love for him? Don't you think it will get too late to confess? What if her girlfriend marries him in the future than what you will be doing?"

Shanaya replied, *" I never want to snatch him from his friends or family, I like him, and I am not some thief who is going to steal him from the world and he is committed this is not the right time to confess my emotions to him ." Shanaya and her three friends Sami, Mayera, Riya* even had a meeting at home just to discuss all this before the date 22nd October.

Those were the happy days of her life, as she had a crush on Aarav. She could never understand her feelings for him whether it was some kind of infatuation or attraction or she was actually in love with him. From morning to evening her only work was to think about Aarav. Her small world used to start with him and end with him. The whole class started talking about her and Aarav. Shanaya got a piece of news... breaking news. Aarav and his girlfriend had a breakup one month back. She was shocked after hearing this statement from Aarav when he was sharing this with one of his friends. Shanaya was somewhere happy in her heart. She decided to confess her feelings to Aarav as soon as possible.

Chapter 10
The forgotten Voice and Truth & Dare game

Their group including Shanaya, Aarav, Mayera, Sami, Ryan, Riya and Salvi they all loved to play Dramsharas, Ludo, current pass, truth, and dare during recess and free periods. Finally, the most awaited day had come. It was the 22nd of October. Likewise, other days that day she was entering from the same gate. Shanaya's class in college was exactly on the 2nd floor in the left row. When she reached the door of her classroom her eyes got stuck on a guy, who was wearing a white grey dotted formal shirt. Her eyes forgot to blink as it was the same shirt that she observed on her day of enrollment in the college. She remembered that when she turned to see him that day, what all could come to her observation was a formal shirt. This shirt was worn by the one with a mesmerizing voice. The same voice which took her heart away, which was full of attitude and confidence. She was amused to see him again, and the person was sitting showing his back to the entrance door of her class only. She could not believe that he was one of her classmates only, and felt so weird that she could not find him till now.

She got a chance to see him when she almost forgot about him. She could not put a step forth, her limbs were trembling with excitement. She tried to tilt her neck and found out that he was talking to someone over the call. He was having a normal keypad golden-colored cell phone. "It's him? Is that seriously him? Yes, it's him only!! Oh no!!!! Her heart shouted badly!! Having the same colored shirt cannot be a coincidence that too in a very small place. Oh! No, he was the same guy that she had noticed on the very first day of her college with whom she was about to collide. How could that be possible? It was Aarav, Yes it was Aarav. She was dancing like a nerd. She didn't know what it was but she was on cloud 7 that day she finally found 'Her guy' or '**Her dream boy**.' She couldn't understand why she was not able to understand this thing ever that Aarav was the guy whom she heard on the very first day of her college. The voice which didn't allow her to sleep for months was his voice…it was Aarav's voice. She told all this to her three friends Sami, Riya, and Mayera. They all started dancing after the completion of Preeti's Ma'am's Contract law lecture.

That day was very special for her. She and her friends decided to play Truth and Dare after the classes get over as there was a total of 10 people who were ready to play that game. Shanaya was having other thoughts going on in her mind meanwhile the dare fell on Shanaya. Aarav asked her to sing a song, and she sang "Kehdu tumhe ya chup rahu dil me mere aj kya hai". Now it was Sami's turn... "Sami tell us who is your crush"… She took Ryan's name and everybody laughed at her. Now it was Aarav's turn, they all had to decide a dare for him but Shanaya decided to give him something different "Propose any girl out of our group." She had no other thoughts in her mind because somewhere she already knew he was the one whom she was looking for. The one who took her slumber away. And her first crush and her love both were the same people.

He suddenly stood up, and tapped her on her shoulder, and asked her to stand up. She felt so nervous and was continuously thinking Oh God *"What should I do now if this guy will propose to me I will not be able to hide my smile in front of my friends, why he has to do this in front of everybody?? Why?" She started blushing* as she was hell nervous. She couldn't hide her smile. Her face was becoming red. Sami shouted:

"Should I record all this Shanaya? You want it to get recorded?"

Shanaya replied nervously *"No no, not required at all"*, As she knew it will become viral.

Aarav decided to propose to her formally. Maybe he had an idea somewhere that Shanaya likes him. He took a pen from one of the students who were sitting and studying that time in a corner of the first bench. He went on his knees with a big smile on his face and proposed to her with a pen in his hand.

He said " *I love you Shanaya* " Shanaya's world stopped for a moment and she couldn't move from that place. She couldn't react. Aarav laughed loudly, stood up and went back to his seat, and started laughing like insane after completing his dare, while Shanaya was still standing there only and was thinking about all Aarav's formal proposal. Today there was a co-incidence Aarav was wearing the same shirt in which Shanaya saw him for the first time. She went speechless it was like her dream came true. She was smiling she was singing and she was on cloud seven.

(It was not a dream I know It was all reality, yes it all happened in reality today. Aarav Proposed me hurray! Yes, He also loves me yes.. yes.. yes!!!He was looking too cute today …I am so lucky that he proposed to me). These were her random thoughts going on in her mind after coming back to her bench. After that Shanaya decided to leave early for the home that day as she had some plan in her head for the evening.

Chapter 11
The Shanaya's Proposal

On the evening of 22nd October, the same day, Shanaya's parents went out of the station. So she decided to confess her feelings for him. Before sharing them with Aarav, she called Mayera... *"Mayera should I confess my love to him, I don't know what I am going to tell him, and how I am going to gather courage for this? But it's my day and I have to do it by today only! When he can propose to me for completing dare.. then why can't I propose to him for real?*

Mayera replied to her with an affirmative tone, "*Yes! You should go for it..don't waste your time just call him, and say what you feel for him.*" And she hung up the call.

Shanaya gathered all the courage and called him with full confidence.

The moment Aarav answered the call, she started stammering... "Aarav I need to talk to you." He replied:- "*Yes tell me what it is?*"

She replied in a very slow voice "*I like you*" her heart was beating so fast that she could hear her heartbeats very clearly. He replied with a heavy voice, "*I like you too...* took a pause and continued *but as a friend*". Shanaya, *I could sense your inclination towards me earlier. But I am not the perfect guy for you. We both are from different worlds. For me, my freedom is important. I can never stay up in a relationship forever. And I would never want you to feel bad because of me as you are a nice girl and would get so many hearts up for you. I am not the one whom you are looking at. We have nothing in common and as I said, I like you as a friend but I don't feel you like my girlfriend.*" And he remained quiet.

She was broken. Yes, she was broken, tears started rolling down from her cheeks. The signs she was checking from 1.5 years on Google that whether he loves her or not were all went wrong within these last few seconds. All her dreams were shattered, she couldn't move for a minute. She hung up the call. She cried for the whole night. She had no idea why Aarav said no to her. Shanaya was a girl with good features and nobody ever rejected her for her looks or anything. She had a habit of rejecting boys until and unless she could find her dream boy. Today she lost him. she lost her friend, her love, and her dream boy. And yes she was in Love with Aarav madly. That night was long and harsh. She realized her endless love for him that night.

The next day Mayera called Shanaya, *"Shanaya I had words with Aarav about you and him"..she continued... "Shanaya he told me that he is not the right one for you.. he is a flirty boy..he doesn't deserve a girl like you. You should move on. He always knew about your feelings from the very beginning but he wasn't even interested in you* Shanaya replied... *it's okay it's all my fault...I shouldn't have proposed to him."* She completed her words and cut the call. Shanaya after listening to her words decided to remain alone for the next few days.

A week went by, but she was not able to come out of the grief that was sticking her. She was in pain and only the words of Aarav could soothe them.

Shanaya decided to call him again. She wanted to talk to him for once, she wanted to get rid of that heartache. She was not able to concentrate on her studies, unable to eat properly, she refrained from social gatherings. On the contrary, he suggested she should date his friend, Shyam as he would surely be a better partner for her. According to Aarav, he could never be the perfect guy for a sweet girl like Shanaya. His best friend Shyam was a brilliant dancer and somewhere he used to like Shanaya.

Despite giving her relief, he gifted her immense pain, she was shattered and heartbroken. She considered him a humble person and a person with a pure soul. But he came out to be a harsh one. His innocence faded away, everything that she liked about him was making her feel like a betrayal. She started hating Aarav for his statement. This all happened so fast that she couldn't understand anything that was happening to her. She stopped expecting anything from Aarav. She stopped going to college and talking to her friends for the next few months. She wanted to remain alone forever now. She didn't want to see any known faces around her.

Shanaya was a changed girl now. She changed her attitude towards everybody.

Two months had passed away and during that time, Shanaya and Aarav got indulged in some fights on their college group on MyApp. Shanaya was going through a bad phase. She was depressed, Aarav had no idea of this. He never cared about Shanaya.

One day when Shanaya was leaving for her home, a guy Amit asked her to stop as he wanted to tell her something. Amit was Shanaya's classmate and Mayera's good friend. Amit used to like Mayera a lot. He told Shanaya not to trust anybody in the college especially "Aarav", as according to him Aarav wasn't a trustworthy guy. He showed Shanaya's texts of other guys of the class who were interested in knowing shy Shanaya's personal life. There was another guy in the class who also told her the same thing that she should not trust Aarav and should avoid texting him on MyApp. Shanaya now got sure about his nature. She couldn't reach her home that day and stopped her scooty in between and cried for half an hour. She decided to forget him as he doesn't deserve a girl like her.

Shanaya had a lot of ego issues but she never showed them to Aarav, as he was the guy whom she loved a lot. She never accepted the proposals of the guys even during her school days as she was a focused girl who wanted to make her career. She truly believed that there is someone for her and once he would arrive in front of her, she would recognize him with the help of her instincts. Shanaya almost lost her self-respect that night for herself, she thought many times that why she was doing all these stupid things for him. He never deserved her proposal and her love. He was not the guy made for her. Shanaya always had a dream image of her guy in her mind that he should be a sweet person, trustworthy, loving, and caring in nature. She wanted to spend her life with someone who could respect women and moreover, a person with a good sense of humour and level of intelligence. She never had an attraction for Aarav's looks whereas Aarav always thought that he is the best as he looks better than the other guys of the college. Shanaya used to hate this habit of Aarav. He never respected women the way he should, maybe he encountered the wrong girls in his life. Shanaya was feeling so irritated and helpless at the same time. She felt her selection of the guy was wrong. But she forgot that she never selected him it just happened. It just happened without letting her know she just fell for her though she never wanted to. She tried to stop herself a lot but nothing could help her. This was all Shanaya's fault to believe Aarav and her so-called friends and their advice. She was shattered that night, she could never forget that gloomy night. She decided to forget Aarav forever now they will only remain, friends, as they previously were. She decided to kill her feelings for him. Now the thing she needed to focus on was her career only. She wanted to become a lawyer and now she has to focus on this only not on some guy. The main goal of her life was becoming a good lawyer and that's it. That was a long night; a night of self-realization. She slept crying, she made up her mind that all the guys in the world are like him only.

Chapter 12
The Picnic

It had been a few months then, Shanaya recovered herself after that incident. Now Abhikant, Sami, and Shanaya had a group of their own. They all became best friends. They started hanging out together. It was 14th December 2014 when Shanaya got a text on her MYapp, 'Yaariyan group' has added you. Shanaya never had a big group... It was Aarav's thing to involve her in all the outings by especially adding her into all the groups of MYapp. She could never understand Aarav's nature, indeed, he always cared for Shanaya indirectly or directly. But now Shanaya was least bothered about all that, she had harsh feelings for Aarav, as he broke her heart without giving her a valid reason. Now Shanaya was a changed girl.. a girl without feelings and a fake smile. Aarav tried to ask her many times why she smiles so silently she could never tell her how he broke her into the pieces.

They all decided to go to a Picnic in a Park on the 15th of December 2013 as Aarav forced her on the group to join them for the picnic. Mayera, Sami, Riya, Shyam, Ryan and Salvi used to live in a hostel while Shanaya used to stay on rent with her mother and father 35min away from the college campus. They all were getting ready for the picnic, girls seemed to be very excited about the picnic as Aarav was coming. They all met at a decided place and hired a cab, reached the location before time. Aarav was also coming so Shanaya and Salvi tried to look good that day, Salvi also used to like Aarav a lot, they were good friends. Shanaya was also excited somewhere she couldn't understand the reason but she was happy that day. Well, they all met at the decided location, but Aarav found it somewhat boring he scolded the person who made the plan. They decided not to waste their time in this park anymore, they all should leave for the Theatre so that at least they can enjoy themselves over there. This was the time when nobody was having cash as they were students only, even Shanaya was lacking out of cash that day but she wanted to go to a movie after the park with the group so she said *okay no problem* as usual. Aarav always had a leadership quality unlike her. He insisted everyone should watch 'Zed minus'. Shanaya didn't agree with him as she was still angry with him for breaking her heart. She was trying to oppose him for everything. Everyone got agree with him so Shanaya had to say yes to the movie 'zed minus, it was a nice movie but she was not in the mood to watch it. So Shanaya, Sami, Mayera, Riya and one of Aarav's friends Shyam decided to gossip instead of watching this movie forcefully for 2 or 3 hours. Five of them invested their full time in gossiping whereas Aarav and the other two people were watching the movie in the same theatre. They all were laughing and talking. Aarav tried to scold them by shouting at them, but they ignored him. After completing the movie when Aarav came out of the theatre, his cheeks and eyes were getting red out of anger. Shanaya was enjoying this too, as he was looking cuter now. Shanaya was trying to stop herself from looking towards him, but as usual, she was helpless. Nobody could ever ignore him and Shanaya was not different. He booked a cab for the girls and went back to his home without saying a single word. Aarav was a mysterious guy she tried to understand him many times but got failed every time. Now she wasn't interested either in knowing him more. Aarav had a habit of not talking when he was out of the college campus. Shanaya used to feel he had a personality disorder sometimes he was too talkative and other times he was too silent. Somewhere she couldn't forget him. The Day was memorable. She reached her home before 6 in the evening.

Chapter 13
Party and Long Drive

24th July 2015

A few months had passed by. The month of July was plumping the humidity and the summers were at their peak. Shananaya kept herself away from the distractions and focused on her dreams. It was not easy for her to stay away from someone whom she adored the most. She convinced herself that he won't come back to her. She became a serious person and did not involve her in social gatherings.

That day it was the birthday of their common friend and Shanaya had got an invite to the party. She denied attending that citing some stupid reasons. As she was aware of Aarav presence there too. Shanaya's friends insisted, but she bluntly denied it In the evening, her friends reached her home. "Shanaya, don't be a spoil spot dude. It has been so long you have not joined us at any party." Her friends screamed at her. *"No, I am not in a mood to go, you guys enjoy. I would stay at home."* Shanaya replied to them flatly.

One amongst them opened her wardrobe and got a dress for her. They forced her and she had to join them with no choice left. When she came out, Aarav with one other friend was waiting in his car. She was stunned to see him there, he was in the driver's seat and came to pick her from her house despite saying no. She had to go and sit at his back and the car began to fly in full swing.

Aarav owned a black swift those days. He turned on the music and they all were dancing like idiots. Although she was quiet, deep down in her heart she was enjoying that moment sitting behind him. She snubbed her emotions somewhere but he held a secret place in her heart and she was happy to saw him there at her place, she somehow felt connected. She still used to love him but she didn't want him in her life as he had already broken her heart into pieces. That long ride at a speed of 150km/hr was an unforgettable memory for her. She enjoyed the drive and his eyes as they were the best scenic things for her. She loved to notice his eyes when he was not watching her. His innocence was there in his eyes but Shanaya wanted to know the true reason behind his ignorance towards her. She still had those feelings for him somewhere hidden in the small corner of her heart.

It was 25th September 2015, Freshers Party day. Shanaya was so excited as she was going to wear a red dress at the Fresher's party. She particularly bought that dress from Pacific Mall of Dehradun. She knew somewhere that Aarav will be seeing her the same way as he used to see her in the very first year with his open mouth. She asked her father to drop her. He dropped her on the college campus. As Shanaya was about to step out of his car, she noticed another car behind her car. She could feel his presence around her. She understood it was him only. She ignored him and his friends as usual and moved towards the gate. That day, the same co-incidence happened. When she was coming out of the assembly hall he was entering the campus and was standing right in front of her. She avoided him as She didn't know why it always happened with her during her entire college life, the co-incidence of entering together from different gates. Whenever she entered her campus Shanaya always found Aarav standing in front of her and vice versa. They had a sort of soul connection. In fact, whenever Shanaya used to enter the college campus it was her routine to check Aarav's car whether he has come to the college or not That day he was looking handsome in a blue blazer and white trousers and she wanted to compliment him but as he was committed she stopped herself somehow. Aarav was a guy who cannot live alone single even for a day.He always had a girl friend around him. Shanaya decided not to complement him that day instead of this Shanaya got a compliment from him in a unique way in front of her friend Mayera. Mayera told Aarav "Shanaya can't ever do make-up... She is too simple." He replied to Mayera *"Shanaya Doesn't need makeup she always looks good."* After hearing this line from him, Shanaya couldn't stop smiling and blushing. She was again on cloud 7. She wanted to control her happiness... Her desire to get him...But she couldn't do so. She was busy thinking all this meanwhile one of her classmates while hosting on the stage tried to tease her *"Oho Shanaya... Aarav is sitting behind you only what else you are looking for."* As he completed his statement the whole class started hooting. She looked at Aarav, but he left the room with one of his friends. She even asked him to stop that guy who did all this but being a nice gentleman he didn't say a single word to the host. When Aarav had no issues with the guy than Shanaya also went out of the class. Shanaya wanted him to take some of her pics. He asked Shanaya to come on the terrace as all the friends were waiting there for them including Mayera, Shyam, and Salvi. That day he took her best pics ever from his iPhone, he did her photoshoot without asking for it. Shanaya asked to delete all the pics from his phone. Shanaya always had trust issues, she never trusted any guy so far. This was not the first time she did so. It was her nature to doubt guys. Aarav had an iPhone that too he got from his salary. Shanaya had a kind of respect in her heart for him, she could never understand the reason. He was a self-made guy. He never asked his parents for money, she always appreciated him for this. That day they all danced together and the party came to an end. Shanaya was roaming around the campus as the atmosphere was very humid that day. She was continuously thinking about him without any reason. Somewhere she knew that she was still in love with him. She hadn't forgotten him. Shanaya went back to her home that day her brother came to pick her up from the party.

"I always knew one thing about Aarav that he is a guy with pure heart and soul. My choice can never be wrong. A guy who loves animals and who respects his professors, family, and friends can never be the wrong person. He is a pure soul he shows me that he is a millionaire but always fights with his friends for money. I don't mind actually. I love him for what he is, I never want to change him. I will always love him because I have no other option I cannot run away from feelings for him. It is eternal and divine, the sentiment I had for him and the connection we had. I wish he could love me for a minute, for an hour, for a day, or for a lifetime but he never got time from his things maybe I am not that good enough. Why he broke my heart I am still not getting this thing why he did it with me?? why? She was continuously thinking about him on the way back to her home while sitting on the front seat of the car with her father.

Chapter 14
College's Last Day

Shanaya was wondering, "Sometimes I feel like why he never understands my emotions for him. Do I look that bad? Or he wants something else in a girl that I don't have? Why I am not good enough for him I could never understand this thing. I loved him more than he deserves and he broke me more than I could ever expect from a guy. I got uncountable proposals in my life but I always waited for his proposal that never came out of his side. It's still my dream to see him coming with some red roses and a ring in his hand in a black blazer and a red shirt. It suits him like hell. He takes my heart away whenever he wears his black blazer, I still skip my heartbeat while thinking about him in that attire. I first saw him in a black blazer in my very first year of college when he was waiting for me as I had to write his arguments. He got 29 out of 30 marks on that assignment. I used to help him with his assignments and notes in the very first year. From the second year, I stopped this as I wanted him to work hard on his studies but there were many people around to help him out because of his extrovert nature. He is a Magician with a smile he can do wonders. It was not about his looks, it was all about his presence and energy coming out of him. That is my love for him "Pure and Clean". He is not in my destiny I always knew this thing. Maybe he wants someone better than me. He could never fall for me and I could never fall for someone else in my life in these last 5 years the way I fell for him. I still have that passion for him hidden somewhere inside me. I can tell him his list of friends and girlfriends in a few seconds, it's all on my fingertips. His likes and dislikes. I stalked him a lot on Friends book, his Vista account is private I couldn't find him. But Mayera had sent me a lot of Photographs of his friends, girlfriends, and him. I still stalk him sometimes once in 6 months, he removed his ex's pictures from his Friends' book maybe he is too hurt with the girlfriends he had in his past. (These were the random thoughts of Shanaya that often used to come to her mind.)

This was her last year in college. Shanaya went on her summer internship for three months, and once she came back, the illness had caught her for a while. Hence, she was not in contact with Aarav those days. Although they were not having terms like earlier those three months went by, without getting in touch for once.

31st of December, 2017

Shanaya called Aarav to conduct and make plans for the new year's eve party. He had made some other plans but had canceled all of them and came to meet Shanaya with Shyam and Shanaya came with her sister Snigdha. All four of them went to the Pacific mall and watched a movie together, and then went to a nearby restaurant, for some quick snacks and the long chatting and gossipping session… They were having a good time with each other. Shanaya was comfortable with Snigdha too as she had shared her emotions for Aarav with her, and being an elder one she could understand the trauma, her sister went from. Shanaya was heartbroken but she still had feelings for him, and she was happy when he was around. She was trying to look into Aarav's eyes and was trying to make some eye contact with him but as usual, he was avoiding looking into her eyes during the entire journey. He and Shyam were busy cracking jokes with Snigdha they all were behaving like childhood buddies whereas Shanaya was still trying to know the reason behind Aarav's rudeness towards her. She was lost in her thoughts.

"Kash aisa hota ye asman ruk jata…sirf wo aur mein rah jate is dunia me jhan wo mere har sawal ka jawab dene k liy majbur hota.."

She also started imagining her and him walking together holding each other's hands in some moonlight on a beach. Having a cup of coffee in their own home on some hills.

That evening she wanted to speak to him about his thoughts towards her, what made him say no to her proposal, despite pretending to be a caring person. Why he gave signals to her when he was not interested in forming a relationship? What was the thing that made him rude? Or where did she lack? She was intelligent, trustworthy, honest, loving, caring, good-looking, and most of the above she had changed herself a lot, only for the reason that he liked her that ways. Shanaya tried to take the initiative too, but Aarav wasn't interested in clarifying her query in front of his friend and her sister. She decided to call him later that meeting. They clicked a few pictures. On their way back home, they all were enjoying the drive with loud music, chilling winters, cozy ambiance. Shanaya was happy sitting at the back of Aarav who was speeding the car at 150km/hr. She was pinching him from the back signaling to slow down the speed but he was not in a mood to slow down as fast driving was his passion and he was a confident driver. She was in some other world; when incidentally his hand touched her hand; when he took the treat on him showing his etiquettes; when he used to apply brakes all of sudden which made Shanaya came forward and lean on the back of his seat. Soon they had reached near to their house and both of them dropped them and left.

Shanaya was lost in his thoughts after coming home too, her sister Snigdha got engaged in her work. Later Shanaya decided to call Aarav to clarify the things that happened 3years back between them. She wanted to clear every doubt that day only. She didn't want to wait. She called him *"Hey have you reached home*?

Aarav replied, *"Yes I have*, what happened?"

She said:- *"Thank you for dropping us home today, I wanted to talk about something very important today."*

He asked. Tell me, "What it is"?

She got nervous and somehow managed to reply... *"amm it's about the incident that happened 3 years back. I wanted to clarify that now with you. Someone from our class told me that you have shown my screenshots on MyApp to other boys who were interested in knowing me. I was deeply saddened when I got to know that. I was hurt and felt betrayed. I could understand that you were not having those feelings for me but I felt bad on your part once came to know that you have done that. It was unbelievable."*

"Did you show my screenshots to all the friends? I want to know what happened that day. Please give me a clarification." He said shockingly, *"What are you talking about?? What screenshot first of all we never talked on MyApp or something, We were always casual while chatting, and that too happened once in a year, why would I do that? I belong to a good family and I know what it means when it comes to a girl's character. And you are my very good friend, I did not have any reason to make you shame in front of anybody."*

Shanaya was shocked to hear that, and she asked, *"Are You serious? You never showed up my messages to anyone 3 years back when all these things were going on?"*

He said, *"No not at all, and who told you all this rubbish? You should have trusted me, or could have come to me to clarify then only."*

She replied, "Oh shit how could I be so stupid, I trusted that guy.

In between, he said, that he wanted to say something else too. And began like,

"Shanaya, you have always seen one side of me, which is joyful, attractive, full of happiness and optimism. But there is something about me that is unknown to you. Today, I would like to share my other side with you." Aarav began to speak and remained quiet for a while.

After a long pause, he said, "Shanaya, there was a girl in my life whom I loved like anything. She was more than my life for me and I could have done anything for her. But I never confessed my emotions to her. Once I amassed the courage and went to propose to her. She denied my proposal by saying that, 'Aarav, you are a nice guy and I like you too. But you are a person born with a silver spooning your mouth. You do not know what it means to be laborious. I would like to be with a person who would know the true meaning of this life. I would marry someone who would stand on his feet with all the hard work. I am completely fine with living with limited facilities but my man should be self-made.' Since then, I am striving to stand in my feet for her. And there is nothing against you. I respect your emotions but please try and understand my situation as I am already in love with someone who has changed me forever..." And he went silent for a while.

"You could get someone who would love you forever and would cherish your love. And I am not that ONE. I hope you would forget me if anyhow I became the reason for your grief... You would always find me as your best buddy. Take care and stay blessed. Keep smiling, as you look fabulous." And he disconnected the call.

Afterward, she started thinking about all the things that happened 3 years back, "oh shit why I trusted that guy more than Aarav I could have asked him regarding this then only. She was feeling relieved from the burden of her thoughts which made her feel like he was not a good guy, and she had chosen someone wrong as her companion. She had weaved her world with her a couple of times and what not? For all those years she was considering him the wrong guy. She was delighted with her sixth sense which always trusted him, which let her think positively despite his actions. And the confession that he made with honesty made her fond of him once again. Now she was having a feeling of respect for him too (She slept while thinking about all this that night)

7th June 2018

It was their last day in college, and their last paper was going on. From now on, everyone would move somewhere else for their jobs or maybe for further studies. It was a day with missed feelings. Happiness was surmounting as she had achieved her dreams to become a lawyer but from now on, Aarav and his paths would be parting.

After completion of this paper, everyone would gather in the corridor for the mandatory photo session of all the students in the college. Shanaya was standing beside Aarav and looking at him from her side-eyes. She was having tears in her eyes and was hiding them from Aarav. But deep within she wanted to be with him. She was happy that all the misunderstandings had faded away and they were having a better understanding now. Everyone bade goodbye to each other wishing good luck for their future endeavors.

But Shanaya left the college hastily leaving all the friends behind, and all she carried along was the happy memories of the college.

She was shedding tears of sorrow, as she could not get her love, she was pouring her sentiments which were grabbed by the land. She was feeling gloomy as she would not be able to meet him again like the way they used to, she would miss those hang-around, speedy car drives, bike rides, freshers parties, canteen chillouts, and the photo sessions.

On that day she was not only leaving the college for a better future but was leaving the person she would never be able to see or meet in her life again. She would never be able to feel his laughter, his presence, his fragrance, his stupid jokes. He was leaving her forever that day. With all such thoughts in her head, she had reached home and cried for an hour. And her heart pondered such words:

She could have told her about her feelings in a better way while holding his hands. She wants to dance with him once like the way they danced for few seconds in freshers-2013, an unforgettable day of her life. She always wanted to tell him the things she discovered about him, but he never got time for her. He used to call her Laughing Budhha and she used to call him Bhondu. This was a sweet relationship between them. Even if she does not talk to him for years or decades she can still not forget him. It's not in her hands. She doesn't need him to love her back for loving him and yes she was in a relationship with his memories for the last many years and this will remain to continue forever. His laughter, his eyes, his lips, his way of narrating stories and making everyone smile during boring lectures and bringing new creative ideas, and making stupid plans for the outing and adding her into them are something unforgettable. He is the person to whom she can love all her life by just looking at him. Sometimes she feels if she would ever try to touch him he will disappear like a bubble. In fact, she never wanted to tell him about her feelings ever but due to her friends, she confessed her feelings for him on call that night. She still regrets doing this sometimes. She feels she did a mistake by doing this… but that's a fine thing that happens mistake happens..but love only happens once in a Lifetime and never happens again no matter how hard you try falling in love again.

Later…

She still remembered that Chai ki tapri nearby their college campus. She did not like to go there, but for him, she often visited there, as she could walk miles for him. The tapri was just a few steps away from their college's gate. She loved to had chai and Samosas with him and with their group. That group was never her group, but she always tried to join it for him. He was the reason behind her smile during her college days. He was her happiness, he became her pain. She couldn't even delete his number from her cell though she wanted to. Even if she doesn't talk to him for many years she could not forget him. She couldn't stop loving him even if he gets married to someone else in the future or even if he becomes the father of two cute kids. She will never forget him, never It's not in her hands. She felt helpless as he was the first guy whom she loved like insane. She was truly, madly, and deeply in love with him. She never wanted to snatch him from his girlfriend or anybody. All she desired was him to remain happy wherever he was and that's called True Love she guesses. ***She loves him, and will always love him till her last breath. forgetting him was beyond her limits.***

Chapter 15
The twist

Suddenly she felt the goosebumps on her hands and her body shivered for a while. It was 5 am, and she realized that she was lost in her thoughts for the entire night.

It's been around 7 years, Shanaya and Aarav were not in contact with each other. Aarav had become a millionaire, he was having his business of pharmaceuticals spread in different states like Uttarakhand, Himachal Pradesh, Uttar Pradesh, Punjab, etc. Shanaya studied the file in the morning and decided to take over the case of Aarav.

Shanaya was getting ready to leave for the chamber and she was a little late on her breakfast table. While Mohan, her helper, was serving breakfast to her. Shanaya instructed Mohan, to switch on the TV. It was in the habit of Shanaya to watch the current news while having breakfast and before leaving for her work. She shuffled to the India TV channel and kept the volume a little higher.

The news grabbed her attention and she left the piece of sandwich which she was about to gulp. It flashed and the anchor was narrating it like, "Aarav Malhotra, a multi-millionaire who is a familiar name in the pharmaceutical industry, had been alleged for selling the illegal medicines. He had been arrested from his house and he was unable to produce any sufficient evidence that could prove him genuine and innocent. There are very few chances that any lawyer could save him from these serious charges."

Shanaya took a deep breath when she saw how the Police were taking him with the handcuff tied to his hands. A tear rolled down her eyes and she immediately left for her chamber without finishing her breakfast.

That day, no butterflies were flying in her stomach as they used to when she was a blooming bud, there was only space for the fireflies. Shanaya was no more a bubbly and shy girl, she was an independent, powerful, extrovert, stylish, woman who lived alone in Delhi. After completing her LLB from Dehradun, she decided to shift to another city i.e. Delhi so that she could practice her profession in a better way. It's been 7 years since she had been practicing in the Delhi High Court. She was a re-owned criminal lawyer in the city.

Aarav's assistant took the permission to meet Aarav in the jail. Shanaya swallowed her saliva and headed towards his cell. Once she reached in front of the gate of his cell, she saw him crying. She could perceive the sense of humiliation and helplessness in his actions. His eyes were narrating a tale of his two sleepless nights. He was the guy born with a silver spoon in his mouth. The mosquitoes and insects of the jail couldn't let him survive in that place. Shanaya read his file and felt as it was arduous to get bail in such matters. The truck which was carrying the medicines on his name was loaded with illegal medicine was caught by the Punjab police when it was crossing the Punjab border. The truck was registered in the name of his company and the papers revealed that he was the owner of that truck. His company had to supply the medicines to various states and altogether ten trucks in the name of his company. Whoever be the culprit, in that case, the ultimate responsibility was of Aarav Malhotra only. Aarav bought many flats in different states of the country to work smoothly as he never liked hotels for the staying purpose. Now he was in Police custody. Shanaya felt like, time lands you in an alien situation at times.

She could not hold her emotions and face him that moment and preferred to stand a little far from his cell. When his PA got a chance to meet Aarav, he informed him that, "Boss, I tried to approach the Best Criminal lawyers in the city but most of them denied to take your case as the chances of winning is nothing more than zero. But, luckily, we have hope, there is a female lawyer who is ready to fight for justice, she is one of the best criminal lawyers in Delhi.

Aarav felt a bit relaxed, there was a glimpse of hope in his heart. He said to Prateek, "Please, request her to meet me and take me out of this place as soon as possible. You know it was not my fault."

After consoling Mr. Malhotra, his PA left the police Jail as Shanaya denied meeting with him that moment.

Chapter 16
The Epilogue

Shanaya reached the jail the next morning to understand the aspects of the case and that could only be possible when Aarav could help her with the truth. She told the police inspector, *"I am the lawyer of Mr. Malhotra and I want to talk to him regarding the case."*

While she was talking to the police inspector, Aarav could hear a voice that was familiar to him. He was trying to recall but all his efforts went in vain. He made repeated attempts to see the face of the lawyer but couldn't get success unless the lawyer turned her face towards him who was standing right behind the bars.

"Shanaya, is that you? Oh Gosh, it's you, dude..."

"Hi! Mr. Aarav, I am Shanaya Sanyal your, lawyer for this case."

"Shanaya Oh my God! Where were you for so long? Are you mad... why the hell you changed your contact number, where were you? I have been through a lot in the last 7 years." He was so happy to see her, as his savior. Aarav was almost about to cry, but Shanaya was not here to talk about something personal, she started asking the professional questions which were need of the hour, "How it all happened?"

Aarav started crying and sat down on the floor, After crying for around two minutes, he spoke up, "It's my fault I shouldn't have trusted the wrong person in my life. This is all my fault, I was an idiot, there was a partner of mine, I started my own business with him. We made millions together and one day I got to know that he was doing some illegal business without my knowledge. He was using my name for that. He has trapped me, he set up all the processes in the way that if something happens, I will be behind the bars and that is how it happened." He was sobbing while speaking. He held her hands in his hands and said, *"I have got to know from my sources that he is missing from the time since police arrested me. I am completely innocent. Please do save me and first get me out of this place. You don't know how these people are treating me. They are torturing me badly as it is a matter of Narcotics, they will not leave me easily. Please do something about it. Please!"*

"Don't worry Aarav, we will apply for the bail. Everything will be fine soon."

Aarav replied, "Thank you so much, I know you would let me out from this place." She consoled him and left the place within few minutes.

She came out of the Police station, media surrounded her and started throwing questions at her.

Shanaya Sanyal, "Are you going to fight for Mr. Aarav Malhotra's case? Do you think you will be able to bring a new angle to the case? He is a sure-shot criminal, are you going against odds for money?"

"Aarav Malhotra, my client is an innocent person, you cannot declare a person as criminal just by the rumors wandering around. He is an innocent, I will be proving this to the World as soon this case comes to court." Shanaya avoided further questions from the media, and got into the car, and reached her home. There were too many thoughts, running into her head, her life with Aarav during the college days...they used to be good friends, she used to like him she had feelings for him, he never had feelings for her but that doesn't matter isn't it? Now, in this case, he wanted her to save him. That night was long, she was busy thinking about sorting out the case smartly.

The next day she reached the court early and applied for bail. She successfully bailed out Aarav from the jail. Aarav thanked Shanaya, and stared at her for a minute, he was out of words and he left for his house.

2 days later:

Aarav called Shanaya and invited her to his home so that they could discuss the case. Shanaya accepted the invitation and reached Aarav's place by 6'o clock, in the evening. Aarav was curiously waiting for her. The moment he opened the door he held her hand and ask her to come inside his place.

"Shanaya, I am so happy that you are back in my life as a lawyer. You don't know I was searching for you for a few years."

Shanaya was speechless as she wasn't able to figure out anything, her mind was blank. Shanaya said, "Aarav let's not get on to the matters which are not professional, on the first place we have to work on your case, tell me what has happened from the beginning?"

"Okay listen, after college, I completed my MBA and joined dad's business. It wasn't going well, at that point, I and Ankit decided to start our own business of pharmacy on a partnership basis. It was all going well and we became millionaires in 7 years. Everything was going perfectly. One day I got the news that our truck was caught between the borders of

Punjab and Himachal. The police officer caught our truck, enquired the driver, and seized the truck. The next day later police arrested me with a proper warrant. He was doing the business of illegal medicines without my knowledge, and he is the reason behind this critical condition."

Shanaya took a deep breath, "Okay! You provide all the necessary information along with your documents, we need to draft a solid case because the chances of winning are less, but I am optimistic about it and taking this as a challenge." Soon, Shanaya waved goodbye and left his house.

She filed the case in court the very next day of coming back from Aarav's house.

Shanaya worked hard on the case, and going deeper into the case, she found out some shreds of evidence that were proving him innocent. She submitted all the proofs and took him out, innocent and honest. She did all that within 6 months and few hearings. She won the case.

Shanaya was happy after winning the case and she received an invite to Mr. Malhotra's party in the 5-star hotel. Shanaya only liked two colours in her life either white or black, but she chose to wear red that day. As the colour was perfect for the party purpose according to her mindset. She reached the rooftop restaurant by 8 PM. She was looking elegant in a red gown than ever before. That evening so many business delegates were there at the party. Mr. Aarav was talking to his friends about Shanaya and was praising her in front of his friends. Aarav's family was also present at the party. The moment she steps into the restaurant, she could see, red and white balloons all around; beautiful romantic music was being played "me tujhse hi chup chup kar tere ankhein padta hu kon tuje yu pyar krega jase me karta hun". Thousands of candles were burning all around. She asked the waiter where is Mr. Malhotra and he pointed his finger towards him. The moment she tried to move towards Aarav, he started coming to receive her. Before greeting each other, Aarav suddenly held her hand and kneel before her. "Shanaya thank you so much for making me win today, you are the person who saved me from the worst. Thanks for everything, let me come to the point, I remember you used to like me during our college days. That time I couldn't say yes to you as I was in a relationship with someone else. It was all my fault. Sorry!! Please accept my apologies and WOULD YOU PLEASE MARRY ME?"

Shanaya went in shock. "Aarav see it's not possible now, I can't marry you ever." She tried to lose the grip of his hands with the tears in her eyes.

She wanted to run away that moment only but did not want to insult his family or hurt his emotions. She chose a dark corner to stand as she wasn't feeling good. Aarav tried to follow her but someone came from behind and congratulated him. He wanted to confront Shanaya, but he had to talk to that person. After a while, he reached that corner where Shanaya went, but could not find her there. He felt something was wrong, where is Shanaya. She was nowhere. He looked for her everywhere and all of sudden, screamed, "Shanayaaa...." Everybody rushed behind him and gathered at that place.

The body of a girl wearing a red gown could be seen lying on the road. Aarav started crying after seeing the dead body lying in front of his eyes.

A shadow was seen running behind the bush...........

...........to be continued